Rattlesnake's Relay Race

by Laura North and Leo Antolini

FRANKLIN WATTS
LONDON • SYDNEY

Franklin Watts
First published in Great Britain in 2016
by the Watts Publishing Group

ISBN 978 1 4451 4782 6 (hbk)
ISBN 978 1 4451 4784 0 (pbk)
ISBN 978 1 4451 4783 3 (library ebook)

Series Editor: Melanie Palmer
Series Advisor: Catherine Glavina
Series Designer: Peter Scoulding

Printed in China

Franklin Watts
an imprint of Hachette Children's Group
Part of the Watts Publishing Group
Carmelite House
50 Victoria Embankment
London EC4Y 0DZ

An Hachette UK Company
www.hachette.co.uk

www.franklinwatts.co.uk

FSC
www.fsc.org
MIX
Paper from
responsible sources
FSC® C104740

The relay race
was about to start.

"GO!" The first runners
were off. Team Parrot
made a flying start.

Team Porcupine raced
to the front.

Team Octopus tried to catch up.

Team Rattlesnake were last. But they had a plan.

On the final lap, Team Parrot were in third place.

"Pass the baton!"
Parrot squawked to
his teammate.

Suddenly Rattlesnake slithered faster. He opened his mouth wide.

GULP!

In went Parrot.

"Squawk!" cried Parrot,
"Let me out!"

"No way!" hissed Rattlesnake, "I'm going to win."

Rattlesnake went faster.
He caught up with
Porcupine.

He opened his mouth wide. CHOMP! In went Porcupine.

"Squeak!" cried Porcupine.
Rattlesnake burped.

Octopus crept past. He was nearly at the finish line.

FINISH LINE

Rattlesnake went faster.
"Squawk!" cried Parrot
from Rattlesnake's belly.

"Squeak!" cried Porcupine.

"You can't fit me in,"
said Octopus.

"Oh yes I can," said Rattlesnake. He opened his mouth wide.

SLURP! In went Octopus.
"Let me out!" he cried.

"No chance!" hissed Rattlesnake. "I'm going to win."

FINISH LINE

Rattlesnake raced to
the finish line. His team
were cheering.

Suddenly Rattlesnake
let out a huge BURP!

Octopus held out
his baton ...

27

"Team Octopus wins!"
shouted the judge.

Rattlesnake was angry. He opened is mouth wide ... but Octopus stopped him!

Puzzle 1

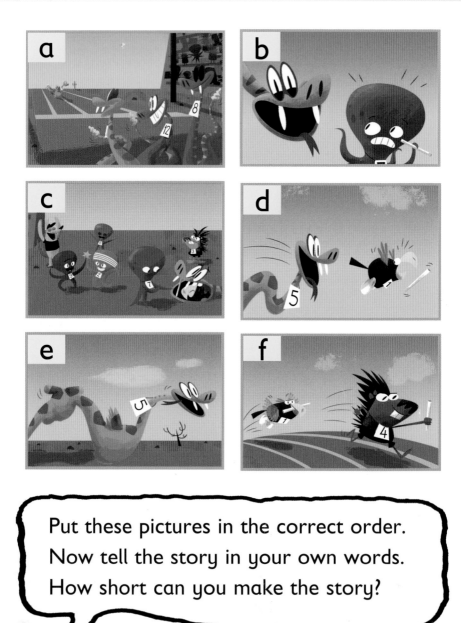

Put these pictures in the correct order.
Now tell the story in your own words.
How short can you make the story?

Puzzle 2

cunning   helpful
greedy

fast   lazy
spikey

Choose the words which best describe the characters. Can you think of any more? Pretend to be one of the characters!

Answers

Puzzle 1

The correct order is:

1f, 2d, 3e, 4b, 5a, 6c

Puzzle 2

The correct words are cunning, greedy.

The incorrect word is helpful.

The correct words are fast, spikey.

The incorrect word is lazy.

Look out for more stories:

For details of all our titles go to: www.franklinwatts.co.uk